Jazzy

Jazzy

By

TL KATT

A story from the Winter Thrillz Collection.

This book is a work of fiction. Any characters or events are purely figments of the author's imagination.

Jazzy

Copyright © 2019 TL Katt
ISBN: 978-1-951017-04-0
Cover Design: TL Katt
Editor: Dawn Lewis

Published by Books by Elle, Inc.
225 College Dr. #65504
Orange Park, FL 32065
www.elleklass.weebly.com

Chapter 1

I wrinkled my nose as a burst of exhaust fumes eased into it. The two cars beside me were closing distance so I quickly made my move and veered my car into the lane, squeezing between them. I always missed the turn, even after following the same route for the third time this month alone. The driver behind me grumbled as he flipped me off and honked on his horn, but I made it into the tight space and made the left turn onto the familiar road. The trees rushed past as the mass of flowing traffic surged forward at speeds exceeding fifty.

A few miles down, I pulled into the right-hand lane and followed it around to garage parking. This part of the trip I never messed up. On instinct, I ducked my head as I entered the parking garage, reminding myself the roof in my car didn't shrink and I should sit up. Straightening my back, I fought the urge to keep ducking as my car climbed the winding path until I spotted a free parking space. As a bonus it was close to the elevator that would take me on the catwalk to the airport.

The muggy Florida air hung like suspended water droplets, coating my already sweaty skin even though it was December. The air conditioner in my car quit working last week; due to limited funds and time I hadn't gotten it fixed. In Florida, when people buy cars, the one thing they're concerned about is the air. Forget new tires, brakes and leaky hoses; air conditioning was a must.

Cool air covered my sweaty skin, causing me to shiver as I stood in the line to check in. As I reached the counter, I handed the lady my license and said, "To Atlanta Georgia on the 5:35 flight."

Jazzy

She glanced at it from under her glasses. "Jazzilynn Spencer?" she said in a question.

Jazzilynn was my legal name that I always used on airline tickets or anything legal but nobody, including my teachers throughout school, ever called me by it. I was always Jazzy. I nodded a yes.

She placed her hand on the keyboard and scrolled, making sure to touch with the tips of her fingers and not her dangerously long fingernails, sharpened to points like tiny little daggers. Her brows arched and forehead wrinkled as she mumbled to herself.

"You said Atlanta?"

"Yes, is there a problem?" I didn't have time for this crap. Atlanta was an almost six-hour drive and I needed to be there within three.

"I don't see your name. Have you ever been married, maybe booked it under a different name?"

"No."

"Let me try something else." She clicked more buttons as I waited.

A few minutes later, someone else showed up and they ogled the screen then peered at me. "I'm sorry, but you're not on this flight and it's full."

My mouth dropped. There was no way. "I booked it last night and it was half full. There's no way!"

She swiped her long auburn bangs from her eyes, displaying enormous amounts of boxy blue and lavender shadow. "I'm sorry, there's nothing I can do."

Then I remembered the confirmation emailed after booking. I pulled my phone from my purse and opened my email, hoping my 4G wouldn't bug out on me. Luckily it didn't and I found the email, stuffing it in front of her face.

I watched her eyes with their outdated makeup move from me to the phone. She cleared her throat. "I can book you on the next flight and put you on standby for this one. If anyone misses their flight, then you get the spot. It's the best I can do."

The best? I bought a ticket and am being denied its use? "I have a funeral to get to!" I stressed. Rage and anxiety swirled together as they rushed up my spine. Water glassed my eyes and soon large crocodile tears burst forth and dropped onto my cheeks. Jacob's face splintered in my mind. He'd always had my back. It was my turn to have his.

I reached over the counter, oblivious to what anyone around me was thinking or saying and grabbed for my driver's license. Bad Makeup Job swatted at my hands as if I couldn't retrieve my own property. I swatted back as I snatched it then stuffed it into my purse and backed away, one slow step at a time.

I had a decision to make, either get in my car and make the near six-hour drive to Atlanta, sweating like a sweet tea on a summer day, or wait. Neither was going to save Jacob. I shuddered as another wave of emotions washed over me. I'd drive. It was my best chance to get there.

A deep voice from behind me said, "Miss Spencer, I need you to come with us."

I turned to see a tall man with a build as thin as the blond hair on his head. He looked like he'd fall over if I pushed him. A firm hand grasped my arm before I had a chance to respond.

I turned my head. The firm grasp belonged to a large man. His polo shirt did little to hide that his chest was bigger than mine, only all muscles. "What?" I asked through my tears.

The thin one restated his request as the strong one pulled me along. It wasn't that I was given a choice. White paint covered the walls and plastic chairs, resembling the kind seen in all public schools across the country, were in the middle of the tiny room. The strong one released his grip as the other closed the door and twisted the lock.

My tears dried up as rage alone filled every pore in my body. "First I'm kept from my flight and denied being at my friend's funeral. Now I'm locked up with stick fry and block," I spat.

"I understand you must be very upset and confused, but we need you to answer a few questions. Do you have a sister or a female cousin that you resemble?" said the thin one.

The strange question took me aback. "Why?"

"I ask the questions, not you."

"I don't know what's going on." I dumped my purse on the floor. "There's no weapons. You have no grounds to pull me back here. I want to leave now!"

The thin one sighed. "You fit the description of someone we were warned not to let on the flight."

I narrowed my eyes. "I was denied using a ticket I paid for because I look like some felon or terrorist running around?"

The muscular one stood silent, his arms crossed over his large chest and his firm jaw clamped closed. I wondered if he had a voice. If I didn't hate him, I'd admit he was attractive with his thick dark curls and silky brown eyes.

The thin one spoke again, "There is an alert for this person and if you know something you need to tell us."

"I don't know anything and I'm not dangerous. I am leaving," I stated, picking up my wallet, keys, and lipstick. *My luggage?* I thought back. I'd had it at the counter and even lifted it onto the scale. "I guess you already rummaged through my luggage and found it is only filled with clothes."

The thin one nodded. "It's been cleared and is waiting outside the door."

"Did you have fun going through my

underwear?" I huffed as I twisted the knob, breaking the lock, and strode down the eerie white corridor, wheeling my luggage behind me. I didn't turn and look but imagined the looks on their faces when they realized their little lock couldn't keep me inside.

Chapter 2

I followed the corridor the way they brought me. When I came to the door, I pushed it open, knocking it off its hinges. The beast inside me was loosed. People talked and bustled about unaware of anything but making their flights.

As I stepped back into the muggy air, I took a deep breath and continued my pace until reaching my car. They'd follow me and were probably watching me on security cameras. I didn't care; let them follow me. They'd messed with the wrong girl in ways they would understand before the night was over.

The trees, grass, and buildings whizzed past me as I drove further away from town, hauling my ass at speeds exceeding my car's limit. It didn't appreciate that. *I'm coming Jacob, hold on,* I thought, hoping he heard me. I felt nothing in response, a void.

I am a majestic or, in layman's words, an alpha female. A panther who will one day lead the few panthers left in Florida. We live under cover in our human forms, hunting at night in the vast wilderness and wetland areas that remain. Our enemy isn't the humans. They are simply in the way, annoying and completely oblivious to the battle that's been waging for centuries now.

I wasn't on the road an hour when I noted head lights behind me. Through my superior vision I kept one eye peeled to the car as I hit I-16 W. Pushing my car to its limit, it flew over the pavement on the near-deserted road. The car continued to follow, so I slowed and veered off onto a back road and then another even less-traveled one, until I was deep in the woods somewhere between I-16 W and Atlanta.

I didn't doubt all of this was due to our mortal

enemies: the jaguars. The battle was over territory. As our inferiors, they weren't as strong physically and couldn't change when they pleased as we could, but they did adapt better into society and into high-reaching places of authority.

I flipped the lights on as the last of the sun's light dropped below the horizon, following the roads deeper and deeper into the woods. The headlights behind stared like two eyes in the night, hunting me. Steering my car onto a grassy area, I left the lights on and crept towards the trees, my movements as seamless as the gentle breeze. Crouching behind the trees, I waited.

All this was taking precious time, but Jacob would understand. A black SUV passed. About a mile down, its headlights went out. Being nocturnal, I didn't need light to see three large men step out of the vehicle armed with semi-automatics.

Blowing out a disgruntled breath, I waited in my spot, blending with the trees surrounding me. They weren't jaguars because they didn't carry guns, always ready to take us on in hand to hand combat. Their clumsy footfalls told me they were human.

Guns poised; they circled my vehicle. One of the bulky men, his wavy brown hair and silky eyes giving away he was the attractive block man from the airport. A second one with a smooth, bald head and muscles exploding from beneath his shirt glanced toward the other men who confirmed a yes nod. Another one with tattooed sleeves strode behind him and perched with his gun at the ready. Even a semi-automatic only served to slow us down. Normal bullets would eventually fall out, rejected by our bodies.

I grabbed a small branch resting by my foot and hefted it towards my car. It hit the roof and dropped. *Darn, another dent.* They tilted their guns, poised to shoot when the bald one said, "It's just a branch."

Tattoo squared his shoulders and dropped the gun to his side. "Think she's gone? Car trouble, maybe?"

The bulky man from the airport punched his brows and followed the tree line with his weapon. "No, she's hiding, out there." *He speaks! Just when I thought he was mute and damn he's clever!* I thought sarcastically. He cocked his gun to point into the woods.

The three men split up and stalked towards the tree line. I could take them out pretty easily but I'd never know what was going on. Why they were following me and why I was denied my flight? That still angered me, not only because it was Jacob's funeral, but I'd spent a fortune on a last-minute ticket. Heat rose through my veins, pumping, my cat attempting to force its way out. *Deep breath, calm down.*

My ears soaked in their movements. Tattoo had harder footsteps and Baldy's were more labored, as if he'd suffered some type of knee injury. The bulky man from the airport had the most graceful steps. He was also the smallest of the buff gang.

Tattoo stalked towards me. His semi-automatic only a few feet from my face as he dropped his shoulders to avoid hitting a large, twisted branch. His eyes shifting side to side as he searched for me.

Forgive me Jacob. I picked up my feet and sprinted through the trees, my footfalls crashing against ground litter as I purposely stepped on every pile to grab his attention. I'd let them catch me. I wanted, no needed, to know for myself and my fellow panthers why they were after me.

Shifting his gun towards my direction he shouted to his buddies, "Over here guys!"

They weren't supernatural by any means with all the noise they made and shouting like that was plain stupid. Woods housed cougars and, on occasion, a passing wolf pack. The panthers and cougars coexisted as allies, as the jaguars were greedy bastards and were attempting to move into Georgia territory as well.

This wasn't a battle between shifters, but something else. Soon three sets of feet pounded the ground, wet leaves squishing beneath their shoes as I swerved between trees. I couldn't let this whole chase appear easy, so I dropped, tripping over a tree root when I heard Baldy only feet behind me.

Jazzy

Scraping to stand, I clutched the dirt and litter then turned my head. His gun was pointed towards me when Baldy's voice boomed through my ears. "Got her guys!" I scooted backwards, my eyes wide in fear, and scrambled to my feet, tossing the dirt in my hands towards him and took off again as if in fright. "Damnit!"

Tattoo and the bulky airport guy were closing in on me. I staggered through the trees, running straight for Tattoo, turning my head from time to time to peer at Baldy as if I didn't know he had friends. I felt like a dumbass scared girl in a bad horror flick.

Tattoo blocked my path with his wide bulk, the barrel of his gun pointed at my face. "I got you." He reached for my arm and I pulled it behind my back then swiveled my body and gulped hard as Baldy and Bulky closed in on me.

'What do you want?" I panted, my voice shaky. My body in a defensive stance.

Bulky stepped forward as if he was the leader. He lowered his gun. "We need you to come with us." His deep voice rattled my inner senses into a frazzle. *Damn, he was hot!*

I shifted my eyes from him to the others and back to him. "You're the guy from the airport. I didn't do anything wrong. What do you want?"

Bulky glanced at the other guys and gestured for them to lower their weapons. "We're not going to hurt you, but you need to come with us," he urged, his silky eyes catching the moon's light. It was almost a full moon.

"You have guns. I have no weapons." If only they knew the strength in my jaw, the sharpness of my teeth and claws. "I'm defenseless."

Bulky shrugged and let out a low chuckle as if I was a simple, defenseless female. I threw him a death glance. "You think it's funny, preying on women alone in the woods, after being denied their flight?" I narrowed my eyes at Bulky to intensify my words.

Tattoo and Baldy grabbed hold of my arms and dragged me out of the woods. I put up a believable fight, tugging my hands and kicking at their shins. I freed one arm and jerked the other almost free of his grasp. He clutched firmer as it slid through his sweaty palms. His fingers digging into my flesh. "I'm not who you think. I don't know anything," I whimpered through conjured tears as Tattoo wrapped his thick hand around my arm again.

As they stuffed me into the SUV, a small breeze

rustled the treetops and brought an odor. It was too far for me to be sure, but it brought back a case of Deja vu. Bulky pulled my hands behind my back and my feet together then wrapped them with plastic restraints as if I couldn't snap free. That was good. It meant I truly wasn't bound and they didn't know I wasn't anything other than human.

Chapter 3

*T*he idea I'd been in the same situation before made the hairs on my arms hackle. I took in my surroundings; the restraints would be easy to break when the time came and it would. Tattoo steered the vehicle, Baldy riding shotgun, and Bulky next to me. His gun lowered on the floor by his feet. The locked door to my right wouldn't take much effort to break.

I glanced at the hand marks on my arm, left by the men. They were already healing, barely a sign of how tightly they grasped them.

"Hell!" Baldy shook a cigarette out of a pack, unrolled the widow and tossed the empty package out. I hated litterbugs. Assholes like him were the reason we were losing valuable hunting and hiding grounds.

"Thought you quit that shit," voiced Tattoo, obviously irritated.

Baldy lit the cigarette, inhaled and responded, "The gum didn't work. Stop riding my dick!"

Bulky scrunched his face in irritation. "Stop quibbling!"

Smoke from his burning cigarette filled my

nose, leaving a stale taste in my mouth. The cool breeze from the working air conditioner felt good against my skin. I swished my lips and glanced at Bulky. From his position, his broad shoulders were straight and square, accentuating the muscles in his chest. *He looked good enough to eat! He's human, what are you thinking?* I knocked the thought out of my brain. I never indulged in sex with humans, even brawny ones. It wasn't safe. Which left me with supernaturals.

The pickings were getting slim as the populations in Florida moved out of the urban areas and into the wilderness and swamps where they could roam freer and hunt without risking the chance of getting caught. Those of us who remained frequented Pizzazz, a bar for all supes. No matter the battles amongst us, when there we had to obey one rule: *truce*.

My last sexual encounter, almost a year ago, was with a panther I met there. It wasn't the best and left me unfulfilled as he'd drunk more than his share of liquor that night.

Baldy flicked his butt out the window and rolled it up. A strong dose of the scent, something like black licorice, wafted through his window as it reached the top. It was getting stronger, closer. The men didn't notice anything as they talked, but for me there was a memory at the edge of my mind.

"So, hey, you have names?" I asked. My little made up ones were beginning to bore me.

Bulky narrowed his eyes and glanced at me. His irises roved my body. "I'm Matthew. I go by Matt. Driving is--"

"What the fuck is that?!" Tattoo slammed on the brakes. As the vehicle swerved, I caught a glimpse of a massive dark object in the road.

The SUV skidded into the dirt on the shoulder,

kicking up dust. Through the back window the object elongated as it stood on two legs. I stared unblinking as it snarled and roared. Its sharp teeth glistening in the moonlight and a long snout wrinkled as it snarled at us.

Its paws thicker than my waist and body as wide as the SUV. It thumped towards us; heavy footsteps hit the road and pounded inside my ears. A black bear and by no means an ordinary black bear or shifter. Its size alone meant something far more. The unsettled feeling and Deja vu kicked my ass and begged me to remember. The licorice odor filled the surrounding air in the cabin.

Tattoo thrust his door open and grabbed his semi-automatic, followed by Baldy and Matthew. These men, for whatever reason they "kidnapped" me, didn't need to lose their lives. "Stop! Keep driving as fast as you can!" I urged, grabbing Matthew's shirt. He shrugged me off as if I was nothing more than a normal human woman.

The men didn't even glance my way as they ran toward the bear with guns blazing. They sunk rounds into it yet the bear continued galloping towards them, round after round dropping off it like it was made of armor.

Jazzy

Tattoo backed up, sinking yet another round into it, bullets dropping onto the road with a ping, the bear swiped its thick arm across his chest. Its claws tore his shirt and into his exposed chest. It then flung him into the air like a toy doll.

"Fuck this shit!" Baldy dropped his semi-automatic and turned on his heel and ran into the dense woods.

The bear roared and gnashed his teeth then hurtled himself forward, dropping Matthew to the ground where he fell and skidded along the cement, stopping beside the open door he stepped out of.

"In... the... back," his raspy breath brought me out of the trance I'd been in watching this colossal, unbreakable beast thrash the crap out of them. *What the hell was this thing?* Our eyes locked, lying on the ground unloading his semi-automatic into the chest of the beast. As if bullets could harm it. The bear's thick arm grabbed the weapon and pushed it into his chest.

He was so helpless, all his muscles and bullets wouldn't do anything to save him, not unless they were sterling silver. "The... back," he repeated, locking eyes with me as he attempted to push the beast off him. My cat felt his pain;

it couldn't watch him be destroyed. Claws distended from my fingers, my snout lengthened. The twisty-ties snapped and the tearing of cloth plunged into my ears as the rest of my body followed suit.

Matt's eyes widened as he gawked at me. I leaped out of the vehicle, onto the bear's back, digging my sharp-as-daggers claws into it and hitting metal-like skin. I pierced through it and it roared in anger and swung to throw me off but I curled my claws beneath its metallic skin. I fought to keep my grip as he thrust from side to side to shake me off.

He growled in pain then plunged his back towards a tree. Its bark breaking against my back causing pain to shoot up my spine. My back paws lost their grip. Using the tree for leverage, I dug my way further upwards towards his neck and sunk my teeth into it. He roared and swung me off him, blood coating my snout and dribbling onto my chest.

He galloped away from me through the woods. Branches cracking against his enormous mass. He was gone for now; wounded, but he'd be back. I had to get Matt and we needed to leave pronto. Shifting into my human form I ran back to

Matt who stood beside the truck, a rifle in his hands, cocked towards me.

"What the hell are you? And what the fuck was that thing?" The gun unsteady in his shaking arms. The fabric of his shirt tattered, exposing signs of his bloody struggle.

What an ungrateful piece of crap. I save his life and this is what I get? "A thank you is in order, don't you think?" I didn't hide the sarcasm in my voice.

"Yeah, okay. Guess I owe that much." His words filled with insincerity and his eyes roved my naked body.

"You can at least act like a gentleman and not gawk at me," I seethed.

He raised his eyes away from my body and met my face.

"I am what I look like and I have no idea what that thing is. What I do know is I only wounded it and it'll return. We need to get out of here now." I stepped towards him then reached for the gun, pushing it out of my face.

"I'm not getting paid enough for this shit!" He dropped the gun to his side and limped towards the SUV.

I climbed into the back seat and collected my clothes. "Damnit," I muttered, witnessing what was left of my jeans. Luckily my cowboy boots weren't harmed. My shirt bore a rip straight down the middle. I put it on backwards, watching Matt in the rearview. His eyes took turns between me and the road, not that it mattered he'd already seen my rack.

"Why switch up to the rifle?" I asked as I clambered half-dressed into the passenger seat. The rifle resting upright against the center console.

He shrugged, his eyes taking me in. "I was told to use it in the worst situation. This seemed like that situation."

"Do you mind?" as if I needed his permission.

"You saved my life so guess I owe you

something." I rolled my eyes. *Why couldn't men admit every so often that women weren't helpless?* Egotistical asshole. I opened the chamber: silver bullets. No surprise there. "Looks like whoever hired you expected this."

He furrowed his brows. "What?"

"The rifle isn't loaded with ordinary bullets, but silver. The only thing that can hurt or kill a supernatural creature."

"Such as you?"

"Don't get any ideas. I could easily rip your throat out before you had a chance to fire the rifle." I closed the chamber and laid it on the backseat, next to my ripped jeans. "It'd be really great if you'd take me back to my car so I can at least grab my suitcase."

With one hand on the wheel, he rested the other against the window. "You don't quit, do you?"

"What the hell?! You and your partners kidnap me, tie me up with plastic restraints, throw me in the back of this vehicle to take me who knows where," I snapped, my voice growing louder with each word. "I save your life and don't even have clothes to cover my naked body that you keep glancing at. It's not on display and I at least want my suitcase. ARE WE CLEAR?"

"Very!"

We rode in silence for several minutes until he spoke again. "You don't know me. I don't know you. We'll be at your car in a few minutes."

"Thanks." From the corner of my eye I inspected him more closely. His jeans tight around his generous legs and, oh my. They didn't hide much! *Stop! He's human,* I reminded myself.

"Stop gawking at me," he ordered with a cocky smile.

Shit! He caught my roving eye looking at his joystick confined inside his jeans. I felt my cheeks flush and cleared my throat. "I was checking to see if you were injured. That's all."

"Nothing I won't survive." He swallowed, his Adam's Apple rose and fell sending heat through my veins.

When we reached my car, I grabbed the suitcase. I grimaced. It would be easy enough to leave, get in my car and drive away, but whatever was hunting us would return and come for both of us. *Shit!* I opened the suitcase, pulled on a pair of jeans and a fresh T-shirt, then returned to the SUV.

I approached him, my face dead center with the barrel of the rifle he held. "I already missed my friend's funeral thanks to you," I seethed, my hands on my hips. I wanted him to know exactly how upset I was, feel my wrath. "That thing will come back for us and the only chance you have is me."

"I'm pretty sure I can take care of myself." He didn't lower the rifle.

"Hah! Like you did earlier!"

He squared his shoulders. "I'm the one with the weapon. Get back in the truck."

I grabbed the barrel and, in a movement, faster than his human eyes perceived turned the table and held it against his chin. His eyes widened and brows shot upwards. "Your human weapons can't hurt us. Even with silver bullets your

movements have to be
swifter than ours." I
marched around the SUV.
Clutching the *oh shit* handles
-- I thrust myself into the
vehicle. "You need some
antiseptic on those cuts."

I braced myself against
the seat and pulled over my
seatbelt, clicking it in place.
He shook his head as he
dropped onto the driver's
seat and swung his door
shut.

We rode further into
the thick woods until we
came to a small, square
cabin. There were no cars
and no lights, so we got out
of the truck and
investigated. Plenty of brush
surrounded the cabin but
there was no sign of life. I

tugged the door open. It was empty; probably a hunter's cabin. The woods were full of them.

He found matches and a candle while I searched for a first aid kit. I managed to find a bottle of peroxide, gauze, tape, and towels. I dumped everything on the table. "Sit down."

He let out a deep breath and his nostrils flared as he took a seat at the wooden table loaded with everything I found. He pulled off what was left of his shirt, exposing his bulk. He had a nice physique. Turning my eyes away, I tried hard not to stare as I poured peroxide onto a rag. He flinched and gritted his teeth as I pressed it against the deep gashes in his chest.

My worst fear was that, whatever that thing was, I didn't want any of it left inside him. Bites and scratches of enough depth from a shifter could cause one to turn although, not purebred, they wouldn't have control over their changing and wouldn't shift completely. Unsure if that thing was some type of shifter, it was better safe than sorry. That's why we always killed and not humans. We hunted animals.

Once I was satisfied his wounds were clean, I took the gauze and ran it around his chest covering them. He held it in place as I pulled off a slice of tape. Pressing it gently, my fingers touched his skin and he caught my fingertips in his. "Thank you." This time his voice was honest and sincere.

"You're welcome." I wiggled my fingers free.

He swallowed. "We were hired to bring you to our employer. He said you'd be safe with him. That's all I know."

Safe was a relative word. In front of me was a divine human specimen. My libido raced as I traced my finger around his solid abs, his body shuddered as I stopped short of the button on his jeans. "Safe from who?"

His eyes roamed my curves. "I don't know, but it's beginning to make sense. I thought you were a simple woman not a... What are you?"

My finger drifted upwards. "Exactly what you saw: a panther."

"I wouldn't believe it if I hadn't seen it. What I see now is a beautiful woman." His fingers drifted beneath my shirt and up my ribcage.

I yanked the button free on his jeans and tugged at his zipper. *What was I doing?* It was as if my body was working independent of my mind that begged for it to stop yet it didn't. Soon he was pushing everything off the table and hoisting me onto it.

I had to stop this but couldn't. It wasn't right, yet his touch was electric and his large cock felt so right inside me. *I didn't even like him* I reminded myself, but it didn't work. On autopilot, my hips met his every thrust. Gathering some control of my legs, I pushed him away.

He fell backwards against the floor and within a second I was on top of him. My hands pinning his to the floor above his head. I straddled his burgeoning manhood, swinging my hips in circular movements, taking all of him in. He felt

Jazzy

better than anything I'd ever
sampled and I lost myself.

   I squealed in pleasure
as my orgasm hit its climax.
All my pent-up sexual
frustration released itself.
His ragged breaths in my ear
brought me back.

Chapter 4

I had him plastered against a chair, his face was contorted in pain and red patches covered his chest, abs, and below his throat from the beating I gave him. Like I said earlier, sex with a supernatural was dangerous for a human but the shit-eating grin on his face told me I'd rocked his world.

Easing off him, I stood. "We get a little carried away."

His smile didn't waver. "I could do that every day." His eyes were glazed over as if in an erotic trance. Maybe he was. We were always taught not to have sex with them because it could kill them, yet here he was bruised but alive and thrilled.

I cleared my throat as I collected my clothes. "Round two will have to wait." I sauntered towards the bathroom which I hoped had running water in the shower.

We snuggled into bed but I couldn't sleep in such close proximity to him. His scent recalled our wild sexual encounter and excited me to the point sleep was useless so I got up and planted myself on the couch. Its springs plunging into my back.

At some point I fell asleep and licorice jellybeans rained down like stinky bullets. I'd always hated the smell of licorice since I was a child. The candy assault was followed by a piercing scream through the darkness. I stumbled towards the shouts then was grabbed up by arms with a heavy panther pheromone scent. Arms I knew and loved: my father.

Light stung my racing eyelids as I jolted out of my dream. Panting, I stared at Matthew. The covers tangled between his legs. His round naked ass on display. I blew out a breath and strode to the bathroom, dousing my face with cold water.

Fully awake now, the licorice scent crawled into my nostrils. "Wake up, we need to go. Now!" I pushed against Matt's back until he turned over. His first response was to reach his thick arms around me. I pushed him away. "We don't have time!"

One at a time, his eyes flicked open, attempting to avoid the prickle from the sun. He rose slowly than swallowed. "What?" That's when I noticed the wounds I inflicted on him during sex were nearly healed. They should be black and blue yet were a faded pink like someone slapped him.

Ignoring his sleepy-minded question, I pulled him forward and yanked the gauze off his chest, tossing it to the floor. The deep wounds had shrunk to half their size. *Oh shit!* I hadn't gotten to him in time. Whatever that monster-bear was he was changing into one. *Catch your breath. Think!* Maybe not. I hoped not for his sake. The healing could be something else but what I hadn't any idea.

"Are you deaf?" I shot at him. "We need to go. Whatever it is it's headed for us."

That woke him as he jumped out of bed and pulled on his jeans. Fear was in his eyes and on his face.

Jazzy

Clutching the keys I pulled him, still punching his feet into his shoes, out the door and into the SUV. The morning air frosty against my skin. I cranked the motor, shifted into gear and spun out of the driveway and onto the dirt road. A cloud of dust trailing us.

I knew someone close who might have an idea what was going on or could find out. A witch who sympathized with panthers and cougars. She was deep in the northern mountain range of Georgia.

"Where do you think you're heading? Turn us around," he ordered. *Ha!* One night of incredible sex didn't mean I was his tool.

I pressed harder onto the accelerator. "We're being hunted and I intend to stop it!"

"That thing is as big as this SUV and unfazed by our bullets. What makes you think you can stop it?!" His voice was firm, but beneath was a layer of fear.

"Oh well, never mind. Let's go ahead and let it haul us by our hair to its den where it can eat us alive!" My rage bubbled to the surface. My cat scratching to get out.

"My job is to take you back to Florida, an address deep in the woods where you'll be safe, I imagine, from this thing." His voice calm as if now he was going to try and reason with me.

I swung my head towards him for a second. "I have a better idea. Hold on," I said, pressing against the pedal as the SUV barreled onto paved road, almost side swiping a silver car as I righted the wheel and continued onward.

"What the hell? You're going to kill us!"

"Shut up!" I took a deep breath, suppressing my anger. "You're pissing me off and that's really stupid of you."

He leaned back into the seat. I felt his silky brown eyes blazing at me. We were climbing the mountain before I broke the silence. "Look at your wounds."

"What the..." His words dropped off.

"So, you don't usually heal so quickly?" I let the snark in my words creep out.

He shifted around in his seat as he clutched at his chest. "This is a bad dream." I felt the heat in his eyes as he glanced my way. "A good dream. I don't know. It's not real."

I leaned over, keeping one hand firmly on the wheel and punched him in the shoulder.

"Fuck!" he shouted, clutching the spot I'd hit him. "What was that for?"

Jazzy

"To prove a point. You're not dreaming and that punch should leave a nasty bruise on you, but it won't." I glanced at the clock. "It's a quarter after nine. Let's see how long it takes to heal."

The SUV bounced again over dirt roads as it climbed in elevation until reaching the small wood shack of Missy Aberdene. As far as the human eye could see there was nothing but dense balding trees. The closest cabin was more than twenty-five miles in either direction.

At this elevation, the air was cold and thin. We exited the vehicle and approached the dilapidated shack, wood curled and buckled on the porch. The door swung open to reveal a dark-skinned lady, her white hair tied into a knot on her head and black eyes peered at us. Her sunken form propped on a cane with a golden handle.

I didn't fear supes as much as I did witches. With the lowering of even an eyelash they could crumple me to the ground, depending on how strong they were. Missy Aberdene was legendary and few knew where to find her.

She narrowed her eyes on Matt, studying him, then flashed them at me. "Come in." The door creaked as she pushed it open. My eyes soaked in the room. Shelves lined the wooden walls filled with knickknacks of sorts.

A lonely red recliner sat in the middle of the floor with a twin—sized, neatly made bed in the corner. Matt eyed me. I felt each of his nerves buckle on end as we followed her through the cabin. Her cane echoing with each step against the floor. She pushed a curtain back and staggered behind it.

A small table surrounded by more shelves containing herbs, mixtures, and books. "Sit." She pointed her cane at the chairs surrounding the table. "Why have you come?" She eased into a seat across from

me and propped her cane
against the arm rest.

Chapter 5

I fed her the story about the bear. Her eyes widened and a sly smile crossed her face. "Oh dear." She nodded than tented her hands on the table-top. "It was before my time, but the stories and lore passed from one generation to the next. The Daeva witch coven left a crimson trail as they blazed into the depths of dark magic creating a beast, unstoppable with skin like armor and teeth sharp as nails. He wiped out many of your ancestors before he was trapped in a cage fashioned from iron and inlayed with silver."

She cleared her throat and stood, fumbling through the books on her wall. "The surviving members of the Daeva Coven went into hiding, scared of their own creation. Now it appears he's been loosed." She placed a book on the table opened to a picture of two cats with panther heads yet cougar markings.

"What is that?"

"Rogue cats, abominations. Their father a panther, their mother a cougar. Of different species, procreation shouldn't have been possible. The mixture in their blood made them crazy and they killed Shagra's daughter. The leader of the Daeva Coven. It's her beast that hunts you now. He won't stop until every cat is wiped from the planet." She paused for a second, adding dramatic effect. "On a full moon he can change into any form." Matt and I stared at her, mouths dropped. *Any form?* In one more night it would be a full moon.

She broke the silence and pointed at the cats. "They were the first of the jaguars." She deliberately stretched the *S* in her word and it repeated inside my head.

"That's all great but how do we kill it?" Matt

asked, breaking the eerie silence.

She cackled. "Kill it? You want to kill it?"

"Can we stop it?" I followed with.

She cackled louder then stomped her cane against the floor upside down, the golden handle looping through an iron ring in the floor. She pulled upward, revealing a basement. "Follow me!"

Her frail body climbed down the ladder of steps. Matt eyed me, brows drawn into a V. I rolled my eyes at him then climbed down behind her. He followed.

The dark room smelled of strong herbs. She lit a candle to display the entire area surrounded in tarnished metal, a mixture of silver and something else. My head grew dizzy and I was glad the heels on my cowboy boots were thick.

"Silver and iron to keep him out. I always feared the day he'd rise again and the shifters have always been my allies." She glanced at Matt and pointed to a large metal chest. "Open that, please."

His shoulders squared in defense like he was any match for this little old woman who appeared frail enough but by no means was. Inside her was magic, possibly hundreds of years old as witches lived extremely long-life spans.

The lid moaned as he lifted it upward and propped it against the metal wall with a ping.

"The black felt bag, please." Her calm voice hid the anticipation her actions relayed as her lips curved into a smile and she straightened her back.

"What is this?" he questioned, holding the bag a foot from his face.

"That is what you need to get rid of the beast." Her curved smile turned into one of satisfaction. "There's a vial inside, you must pour its contents down his throat."

Matthew's eyes widened in fear. "It'll kill us before that can happen!"

A quick cluck of her tongue, she responded, "Then you must be careful."

I took the felt bag and we all climbed back up the rickety ladder one at a time. My body eased not surrounded by the metal that could kill it, weakened my senses, and left me vulnerable. I set the bag on the table. I'd assumed Matt was turning into a beast but in light of the information she gave us now I wasn't all too sure. If nothing else, maybe she had a cure before the inevitable change happened. "Can a scratch or bite from the creature turn a human or shifter?"

As if her feet were tired from a long hike she sat at

the table, leaned her cane over the arm rest and raised her legs onto the chair beside her. "He's conjured, a curse, evil, and only one of its kind."

"Sooo, he can't change anyone?" I gritted my teeth awaiting her response.

Her dark eyes grew solid black without a pupil in sight. "No." The black balls in her eye sockets turned toward Matt, beating into him. "Many cats hid among the humans and bred with humans to protect their offspring from the creature."

I opened my mouth to speak and she squelched it with her hand. "I know what you're going to say."

She paused. "Cats can't breed with other species of cats. If offspring are created, they will be as crazed as the twins that started this whole mess but since you are all part human you can breed with humans."

What was she saying? No, intercourse with humans was dangerous. As if in slow motion I blinked my eyes and in the split second in between I saw Matt and I last night as I ravaged his body and he succumbed. "Holy shit!"

Matt's nose wrinkled in confusion as he shifted off the spot against the wall where he'd been leaning. "Speak English! What does that mean?!"

She cocked her head and grinned. "I think you know."

He blew out a breath. The hairs resting on his forehead tented then flopped back against his skin, resting in place. "I'm going to be a cat. Like her!"

Like me? What the hell was wrong with being a cat? My claws distended at his words and I felt my sharp teeth explode from my gums.

"Simmer it!" she ordered me. I calmed my cat, pushing her inside. Speaking to Matt, "You are a cat. Were born one, but after years of breeding, not much panther is left in you."

"No, no, no! You're an insane old lady!" He paced a four-foot spot in the floor.

I think I was getting it. "He was born with panther blood and we had sex last night so my juices bonded with his."

She smiled and dropped her legs off the chair. "Something like that, and each time his cat form will grow stronger."

Sex! Damnit! That's why they didn't want us procreating with humans. Telling us stories how we'd kill them and such. No. They wanted to erase what some cats did to survive, to save their lives and those they loved by making cat-human hybrids and I had to be kidnapped by one. *Damn my luck!*

He raked a hand through his hair. His pacing wearing thin the already worn out wooden floorboards. "This is all bull shit like a bad fuckin' dream. We're leaving now!" He grabbed my hand to pull me out the door with him.

"I wouldn't do that. It's mighty dark out here at night and these mountains are filled with things that can't be explained." She eased out of her chair and rested against her cane.

Smoke billowed from Matt's ears and his clasp on my hand was tight. It turned me on. As an alpha female I needed an alpha cat, strong, authoritative, with a hulking chest, but also submissive to me. I shook the thoughts from my mind, sex would have to wait. She was right, we shouldn't go anywhere tonight.

Chapter 6

Aberdene suggested we sleep in the basement made with the iron/metal alloy she concocted, but I couldn't. It weakened my cat, trapped me. I'd be defenseless if the beast came in the night.

"Wake up," whiskers tickled my ear as Matt whispered into it.

We'd taken the twin bed, she insisted. Lying that close to him my libido went crazy, my panties were soaked, and I'd barely slept a wink even though we turned away from each other. After about an hour he took to the floor. I guessed, based on the way his jeans followed the contours of his cock, that he'd had the same problem.

I gazed into his silky browns then past them to the window and the wilderness beyond. It wasn't pitch black but not yet sunrise. "Let's go."

We crept across the floor and I grabbed the felt bag off the table. He lifted the hefty, thick metal bar off the door and twisted the lock. It creaked as he opened it and the chilly air enveloped us. "You must get him to drink it," Missy Aberdeen whispered as I passed over the door's threshold. Turning back, I glanced at the old witch. A puff of her white hair rested against the top of the recliner and it rocked gently.

"I will," I whispered back and stalked into the not yet sunrise, following Matt to the SUV. He'd planned this little escape as he stole the keys from the pocket I'd stuffed them into. More and more his feline side was beginning to show. *How did I miss that?*

The SUV crept over the dirt road, bouncing from the uneven mottled surface. "Finding this thing won't be a problem, I don't think, but how are we going to get that shit inside it? If I believe her crazy talk."

I sighed. *Why did he have to be so stubborn yet look so delicious?* I grabbed hold of the wheel, showing my strength far exceeded his and the SUV flew through the trees until he squashed the brake and jammed the gear into park.

His eyes dropped, resting on my cleavage. My own gaze drifted to the bulge in his pants as my hands dropped from the wheel and coasted up his legs, rubbing against it. I straddled him, reached my hand below the steering wheel and cut the engine off then pressed the seat button back until we had plenty of room, grinding against his manhood as it grew and felt like it would bust his pants wide open.

I grasped his arms and pulled them over his head then clamped my teeth onto his shirt and tugged it upward and over his head. The head of his cock plunged over the beltline of his jeans and I hurriedly unbuttoned and unzipped them. I wanted so bad to rip them off!

I lowered my head and licked along the length of his swollen member. His hands plunged into my short auburn hair, grasping it as he moaned in pleasure. I suckled along the head and brought it into my mouth as

I tugged his pants loose. Desire coursed through me as he dropped his hands from mine and traced the edges of my body then cupped my breasts.

He was mine! I lifted my head and traced my tongue along his abs and chest, over his stubbly chin, and found his lips.

"I need you now," he said between heavy breaths. His hands dipping below my breasts and into my pants as he tugged to pull them off.

I leaned back and gripped his hands as I licked against his chin and behind his ears. His thumbs circled my nipples, making them grow. Resuming my spot on his lap I ground my clit over his tip, letting my juices run down the side of it. This was my show, not his. He needed to know where his place was.

Warm, wet splashes shot against my clit as precum ejaculated against me. I kissed along his neck, my hands moving over his body as I circled my hips. My entrance over the hood of his cock.

He clutched me and drew me towards him. "You're going to make me cum without even fucking me." His hands clamped on my waist as he attempted to pull me downwards onto his shaft. "Oh my fucking!" He shuddered as cum squirted upwards and dripped from beneath my belly button. His ragged breathing slowed as I pulled away.

"That was incredible," I said, his head against the backrest and tilted towards me as I dropped back into the passenger seat. His eyes drifted to the puddle of cum dripping from his cock and forming on the seat. "What a mess, but shit, you're incredible. I've never… Shit!"

He stumbled over his words as I reached for my ripped clothes on the back seat, tore my jeans in two and tossed him half. That was an act of dominance to show him I was in charge, that I could get what I wanted, when I wanted, and I had self-control.

Once the fog from our rapid breathing dropped off the windows and our clothes were back on I turned towards him with a cocky grin. The sun peeking over the horizon through the window.

He shook his head. "You sex me up and haven't even told me your name." The engine roared to life then he shifted into gear and pressed on the gas.

The SUV spun tires. "Everyone calls me Jazzy."

He rocked it from reverse into drive but the tires continued to spin in place. "It's stuck good. Stay here. I'll push it from the outside, you steer," he suggested as he opened his door and stepped outside. A licorice scent waffled into the cab.

"Matt," I said, reaching into the back seat for the rifle loaded with silver bullets. He didn't respond so I slid my door open and stalked towards the back of the SUV. *Where was he?* My heart caught in my throat.

"Put that down," he said, my heart returning to its regular spot. "I had to take a leak but glad to know you missed me." A smug grin on his face.

"Whatever." I strode around the truck. A metal chain extended from the bumper. My eyes followed it maybe fifty feet to the tree it was tied to. *No wonder!* We weren't stuck, someone chained us while we were hot and heavy. I dropped the gun and extended my claws. One swipe cut through it as the chain dropped to the ground and hit with a clank.

The ground rattled beneath my feet from pounding footsteps, heavy breathing filled my ears and licorice filled my nostrils. I whipped around and there it stood, one arm draped around Matt's neck in a literal bear hug. Matt's head hanging limp. *Not Matt! He was mine.* I picked the rifle up. "I'm a good shot," I warned as he dropped Matt like a ragdoll and walked towards me.

From my position I couldn't tell if Matt's chest was falling and rising. Fear, anger, rage, and hate filled me up as I glared at the beast. My instinct was to run to him, coddle his head in my arms and check for a pulse, but that wasn't going to happen. The bear-beast stood on all fours and rose several feet above me. I would destroy him but there was no way that would happen with brute strength. I was smaller, quicker, agile on my feet, and smarter.

I fired off a bullet. It buried itself into its chest. For a second it halted then continued, teeth bared and saliva coating his bottom lip. My panther filled with rage, shifted to the front. *Oh fuck! Here goes another set of clothes*, I thought as my feline side reared its teeth, head, and finally complete body. A few feet from him, barely out of his reach, I crouched my back and lowered my chest then stepped backwards as he moved closer to me.

I shifted my gaze for a split second towards Matt who lay limp on the ground. My heart ached for him. The bear made the first move in our one-sided stand-off, reaching his long, bulky, furry arm towards me. I took the opportunity to pounce over his shoulder, landing with agility on the ground behind him.

Quickness and agility, I reminded myself. I had that on my side as I bounded towards his back, sinking my teeth in for a large bite before he swung me off him. Whizzing past a tree, I managed to not hit it and landed on all fours with one end of the chain beneath my front paw, giving me an idea. I clutched the chain in my teeth and ripped it off the tree then ran in circles around him faster than his eyes could follow.

He stomped his feet, attempting to loosen it, but only made it worse for him as it got caught between his legs. His sharp teeth bared and snout wrinkled in anger, he roared and swatted at me. The chain tightened around his legs with each loop I made. Using the SUV's bumper for leverage, I pounced into the air sideways askew and skidded to a stop. The chain buckled around his legs pulling him downward.

His arms flailed and he roared loud enough to wake the dead buried in the woods. I watched in horror as the beast fell hard, taking a tree with him then another as his body collapsed into them. *Shit!* I dropped the chain from my mouth and, scurrying onto all fours, ran in hopes of getting out of the trees' path. Branches fell against my back and then a large, solid, bark-rough tree trunk plunked square on my head. Matt was my last thought as the lights went out.

Chapter 7

My eyes flitted open to darkness. After a few seconds they adjusted. The walls surrounding me and the floor was dirt and rock. Stalactites fell with sharp ends and only a few inches of clearance between them and the stalagmites. Water flowed somewhere outside the room, on the other side of the dirt-rock walls.

My hands and legs were cuffed in silver. It burned into them, weakening my inner feline and strapping me solid to the cave posts they were attached to. Normally I could snap them free of the four poster stalagmites, but the silver prevented that. I took in a deep breath; licorice coated my throat and nostrils. *I hated licorice!*

Beyond any shadow of a doubt, the bear-beast had trapped me. My head felt like it was crushed beneath a Mack truck and throbbed, pain shooting through my body. Coupled with the silver, I wouldn't heal. Excruciating agony riddled my body, then I remembered Matt lying on the ground where the beast dropped him. *Was he alive?*

I had to think beyond the constant throbbing in my head. I was completely naked, meaning no felt bag filled with the potion to kill him. I squeezed my eyes, attempting to remember. We'd left it in the SUV. I needed to get back there, pronto!

The stalagmites holding the chain to my cuffs were tall, all but the one trapping my right arm. If I could pull my strength together maybe I could loop it over the top, giving me one free arm. I sucked in a deep breath and gathered every ounce of strength inside me then thrust my wrist upward, stopping just short of the top. I attempted it again with no luck. The chain rattled against it.

Jazzy

Hefty footsteps pounded the cave floor as the bear-beast ambled into the room. He didn't speak a word, his hulking form leaning over me. Bright yellow-green eyes peered down his long snout at me. His black fur shining in the darkness. I held my breath as he leaned further towards my face and studied it.

From the corner of my eye I watched one of his hulking arms swing towards my neck and within seconds a sharp pain stung above my collar bone and radiated throughout me then everything went black.

I don't know how long it was and my mind was fuzzy from whatever he drugged me with when I awoke. My eyes fluttered to stay open and explore my surroundings. After several minutes, I gained full consciousness and noted I was no longer in the same section of the cave.

A small stream ran in front of me. The water glistened as light from overhead shone on it. Small ripples hit the side bank. I was now sitting in an upright position with my arms and legs still shackled in silver to something firm behind me. My back was leaned against it.

In that moment I realized I was still alive. It hadn't killed me. *Why?* The question echoed in my mind. *Why? Was I of some use to it?* Without any answers, I caught movement in the corner of the room. Without turning my head, I side-glanced an opening for a different room and within moments a man entered, striding to a bench carved from the cave rock. I kept my head low and watched him beneath my lashes.

His build tall and slender. A white T-shirt hanging off his broad shoulders and golden waves of hair fell over his chest as he leaned and took a seat on the carved bench. As he lifted his head, yellow-green eyes, as though they were cut from peridot, shifted towards me, centered on me. His long oval face and high cheek bones gave the effect he was carved from a god. He was the most beautiful man I'd ever seen.

"You are awake?" he asked, his voice music in my ears.

Who was he? Since the cat -- no pun intended -- was out of the bag I tilted my head and met his piercing gaze. His eyes sucked me into an embrace, warm and gentle. "Where am I?"

He stood. Our gazes locked as he stepped with bare feet through the stream, water ebbing around his feet and ankles. Even those were perfect. My senses frazzled and short circuited the closer he came.

Finally reaching me, he bent onto one knee, now at my height. "You are mesmerizing. Beautiful beyond words." He lifted a shackled hand and kissed it, his eyes still fixed on mine. His touch stimulated my senses, driving me to wanting him.

I'd never found myself exceptional to look at with my shoulder length dark auburn hair, average brown eyes, and taller than normal height. My curves were decent, but nothing that turned heads. I was maybe too skinny. His words transfixed me as if I was under a spell. "Can you undo these?" I pulled my other wrist upward to meet the one in his hand.

He replaced my hand gently on my lap. "In time."

My reasons for being held against my will in the cave room escaped me. I couldn't remember. All that filled my mind was his beauty and him; needing, wanting him. Desire burst inside me. Something about his gaze, his eyes, begged me to recall a memory.

He stepped away from me. His gaze unwavering as our eyes were glued to one another then he disappeared through the entrance he came through and his spell fell away. Suddenly, I remembered. Those eyes belonged to the bear-beast. Missy Aberdene's words echoed inside my mind 'on a full moon he can change into any form'.

That was it! The moon wasn't quite full the other night, but now it was giving him strength. He was the beast, and his power against my sapped power, I would succumb to him. Thinking quick and garnering my strength, I left myself a clue and carved a word in the dirt *Luna* and repeated it inside my head.

The effort it took forced me in and out of consciousness. My strength was rapidly declining. A scratching sound tickled my ears but I couldn't place

where it was coming from. I
listened in the quiet. There it
was again, above me. I
pressed my head backwards,
resting it on the top of the
stalagmite, and watched the
golden sunlight darken as a
shadow moved over it.

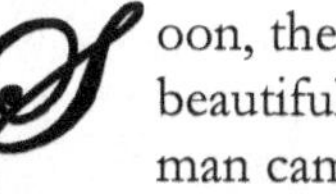

Chapter 8

Soon, the beautiful man came back. I dropped my head and closed my eyes, remembering his entrancing gaze and repeated *Luna* in my mind, over and over. His footsteps, graceful and light, padded towards me. He wasn't in a rush.

I listened and acted as though I was passed out. When he approached, a tiny clink hit the ground to my left like metal striking something hard. A large dose of licorice wafted through my nostrils as he leaned behind me and unlocked the chains. They dropped to the floor with a clink softer than the last, meaning whatever he placed on the floor was in a metal stronger than silver.

His fingers played along my cheeks with graceful strokes then he cupped my chin in his hand. His touch alone drew my senses offline but some capacity remained. "It's time," his voice broke into my head, crossed another barrier, and within seconds all I saw was his beautiful face and piercing eyes, even through my closed lids.

My eyes popped open against their will. There was something I was supposed to remember but couldn't. It clung just out of reach. As my eyes locked with his, it was all forgotten. His fingers traveled over my exposed breasts in circles, sending shivers of ecstasy rushing over me.

They continued down my abs, over my belly button, and played a tune on my clit. Then explored the insides of my thighs and stretched over my legs to my ankles where he unlocked the shackles and dropped them to the floor. "Jazzilynn, you will soon be mine."

Hearing my name brought back a spark of something but it fell away as soon as my mind reached for it. *My name. How did he know my name?*

"You are wondering how I know your name?" he asked as if reading my mind. Running his fingers over my arms he rested them again on my breasts and ran a finger over my nipples. Shivers of delight coursed over my skin. I didn't respond to his question before he answered it. "You are the queen of the panthers. Everyone knows your name."

It was more. Damn, I tried so hard to grasp it. My body reacted to his touch as my nipples hardened and desire for him worked inside me. His hands on my skin wiped everything away and I

Jazzy

forgot what I was supposed to remember. My hands climbed under his shirt and explored his chest. It was firm and soft as silk; taut, toned muscles, yet not bulky. Drifting lower, I found the string that held his pants around his waist and tugged, freeing the bulge forming inside them.

His hands roved my curves and edges, driving my body into an ecstasy that desired him, needed him. He pushed me to the ground, leaning my head against his arm. His tongue nibbling my nipples and running the length of my chest and abs as he gently released my head to the firm cave floor.

A word on the cave floor caught my eye as I tilted my head for him to suckle my ears and neck. It read *Luna*. My eyes shifted upward to the light. It shone from the outside, not bright like the sun but bright enough to be a full moon.

His head now between my legs, his tongue tasting my sweetness. My hands stroking his large member. My body quaked in excitement and desire. *Luna*, I repeated in my mind as if it meant something. His wet tongue against my clit made my body shudder with an orgasm. I clutched him firmer and stroked quicker as waves of pleasure shook me.

He moved upward, his tongue stroking my curves as he lowered himself, his cock above my entrance. I dropped my hand to allow him into me. *Luna*, echoed inside me.

He entered. Moans of pleasure from the thickness of him inside me as it moved in and out, hitting every decadent spot. *Luna*.

Something else, another emotion, one filled with love not lust, caught me off guard. From the corner of my eye a man with short wavy brown hair and silky brown eyes crawled across the floor, something in his hand. I knew him.

A rush of memories filled my mind. The dark-haired man's naked body, his cock beneath my entrance, thrusting myself around it. The feeling of him inside me and the touch of his hands and the full moon. As he closed in on me, I noted he had something black in his hand: a bag. Placing one finger over his mouth to shush me, he opened the bag and took out a bottle. Emptying a chalice, its contents puddled onto the floor. He wiped it dry with his shirt, set it down carefully and dumped its contents into one of the chalices beside us.

Clink. Yes, the golden-haired man had placed them on the ground before unlocking my silver shackles. It all spun together: *Luna, clink, Luna, clink.* His dark eyes. *Matt!* The memories flooded my mind as I involuntarily convulsed in an orgasm while envisioning Matt inside me.

I pushed the man upward, knowing what I had to do as Matt crawled away. I straddled him and ground myself, thrusting my hips from side to side, working his manhood. The next orgasm building inside me was a reaction as I worked him. Visions of Matt filling my mind. I'd play his game.

After several minutes, he rode the pleasure waves surrounding his cock as my vagina squeezed hard, pulsing against him as I continued to work my magic, riding him. His cock throbbed inside me as it was ready to release. In that second, as his mouth opened with his impending sexual discharge, I poured the chalice filled with the concoction from Missy Aberdene into his mouth and snapped it shut.

He struggled against me and Matt hurried to my side and assisted in holding him down until the liquid had a chance to drain down his throat. He coughed and gagged as his body convulsed with spasms. I stood and, taking Matt's hand, we watched.

Jazzy

"What… did…" The golden man's head dropped to the side and his body quit thrashing. The moonlight streamed down on him, illuminating the gory scene. His skin and muscles fell away from his bones. Blood ran over the floor of the cave downhill to the stream and soon flaked.

Matt let go of my hand, escaping to the corner of the room where he picked up a gunnysack bag and, one by one, loaded every bone from the man into it.

"What are you doing?" I asked, grabbing his hand as he closed the drawstring on the bag.

"The bear is dead. I'm bringing this to my employer."

Since magic created him, it seemed magic should trap his bones for eternity. "Why?"

He looked me square in the eye, his soft gaze washing over me. "To free you."

He lowered the bag of bones to the ground and snaked his arms around my waist. His lips pressing against mine in a toe-curling kiss. *He was mine.*

Chapter 9

Matt survived the bear-beast's attack and when he awoke, he drove back to Missy Aberdene's. She used her *hocus pocus* as Matt called it and my clothing to perform a locator spell. Before he left, she warned him of the full moon and its ability to strengthen the beast. He waited, cringing as he watched the beast who'd used the power of the moon to change his form to that of a beautiful, desirable man have his way with me.

He took me to Jacob's grave located on Cougar

grounds. Jacob was a Cougar and my best friend. Because of their trust in me, they allowed Matt onto the property. I laid flowers over his grave, which was nothing more than a headstone. By their custom, they cremated their dead and buried the ashes.

Matt didn't go alone to meet with his employer. I tagged along, after all two cats are better than none, and from our numerous sexual activities since, he was very quickly gaining strength.

He pulled the SUV up to a large house deep in the Florida wilderness surrounded only by trees. Its large, white painted face and thick columns were reminiscent of a plantation home.

"Stay here and stay down," he demanded with concern written across the edges and contours of his face as he pulled up the long drive.

Thrusting the gear in park, he stepped out of the vehicle and hefted the bag of bones over his shoulder. I stayed put and below the dashboard as he asked and used my extrasensory hearing to paint a picture. His footsteps halted as a male voice asked him to stop. I imagined another was there with a pointed gun as I heard three significantly different exhales of air.

He patted him down then slid open the drawstring of the bag. My hearing so acute, I nearly heard his brows crunch in dismay. He pulled it closed, posted his hands to his sides. The door creaked open with the smallest whine. "He's clean," said the same man.

Matt's footsteps sounded from the concrete porch to the tile floor before the door closed. The men outside stayed put, their guns resting to their sides.

"Welcome, Matthew. What do you have for me?" asked a man. From the sound of his voice he wasn't large or tall, average sized and between forty-five and fifty.

The bag dropped onto a hard desk or table, the bones inside clinking. "Take a look."

The drawstring opened. "What are these?"

"I killed the bear. This is what's left. Now Jazzilynn is free and not in need of any protection." Matt's voice firm. He let out a deep breath.

I was more than capable of taking care of myself and hated the thought of *needing* someone for that purpose.

"And so she is. Thank you." He lifted the bag. "I'm keeping these."

Matt's inner cat growled. "I killed it. Those are mine!" I'd warned him of the magic inside them and the possibility of using another dark spell to resurrect them. I felt Matt's anger rise up inside him then heard the crunching of bones as his body contorted into a panther.

Glass shattered, grabbing my attention. I lifted upward to witness a large black panther sprinting towards the SUV. His firm muscles apparent in his stride. The men at the door lifted their guns and fired. Bullets rained down on him.

Jazzy

I pushed my door open and scooted into the driver's seat wasting not a second to fire the ignition as Matt's feline form jumped on the passenger seat, tossing the bag to the floor. I hit the gas. The SUV kicked up dust as it fish-tailed out of his driveway and onto a paved road.

He was mine and I would forever protect him as he'd forever protect me.

Jazzy is one story from Winter Thrillz 2, only available in ebook. Keep reading for the first two chapters of Esma Rose.

Chapter 1

Esma stood at the crosswalk. The light on the other side flashing red. Her eyes fixed on the light until it blurred. She wrestled with her thoughts. *Was she too hard on him?* She and her boyfriend got into a fight. Esma left and now, moments later, stood in front of the red hand light, staring at it.

When they fought it was always petty. *Was she petty and a vain vixen?* He

called her one and it
angered her. She was a
one man at a time gal and
it was important for a
woman to maintain her
youth and always look
presentable.

The street lights
glowed above her, shining
onto her plaited auburn
hair hanging beneath her
white hat. She wore a
long white leather coat
matching her hat and
knee-high mahogany
boots. The chilly air
flushed her cheeks and
nose but she didn't notice
the cold.

Cars beeped and
honked as they zoomed

Jazzy

past while she stood staring at the light. Snowflakes fell softly, dropping onto her and the ground.

"Are you okay?"

She zoomed out of her thoughts and glanced at the man next to her. The muscles beneath his shirt defined enough to see their outline through the loose-fitting button-up shirt he wore. His slacks, made of lightweight material, were crisp and ironed.

His face edged with a strong jawline and his lips full, but not too full. A well-manicured mustache beneath his straight nose. Sandy brown hair streaked with gray covered his head and was neatly trimmed above his ears. But his eyes were his most striking feature. They were a piercing brown that smiled warmly at her.

"I will be," she responded.

He pressed the walk button and the blinking red hand changed to a solid white person. They crossed the street.

"You stood in front of that light several minutes. Are you sure everything is fine?"

She adored gentlemen and thought again of her boyfriend and their silly arguments. A smile tugged at the corners of her lips. "I got into a little disagreement with a friend and now I'm overthinking it."

"You can never overthink a problem with a friend and it's never too late to make everything right again," he stated, walking in stride with her.

"This time it is," she answered with a hint of sorrow.

"How's that?"

Esma ignored his question. "This is my

house. Thank you, uh… I never got your name," she said, brushing a white gloved hand along his.

"Gracen Halinger. A beautiful lady should never walk home alone." He smiled and watched as she walked up the stairs to her house.

She strolled inside and flicked on the light, setting her keys on the small table beside the doorway. She peeled off her coat, gloves, and hat, hanging them in the closet, then shifted and cautiously stepped into the living room. Her boyfriend lay on the couch, his eyes closed and chest still. She leaned close to him and didn't feel his breath. "Honey." She gently shook his shoulder. His arm dropped off the side of the couch, touching her abdomen.

Registering he was dead, she screamed!

Chapter 2

The gentleman didn't hesitate upon hearing her scream and ran up the steps to her home, taking them two at a time with his long stride. He burst through the door, following her screams. She was kneeling on the floor, her brown eyes huge and tears falling across her cheeks. Laid out on the couch was an olive-skinned man with dark coffee hair and a neatly trimmed matching mustache.

He rushed towards her, eying the man. "Is he--."

She cut him off with a whimper, "Yes."

"Call 911," he demanded as he grabbed a poker from the fireplace and stalked the house. The living room led back to the hallway. It was long. Across from him was a dining room. A bouquet of roses in the center of the table set inside a crystal vase. The room was empty and led into a kitchen. The square room contained a breakfast nook and island, pots and pans hung above. All still and clear, he went back into the hallway, peeking into the living room. Still squatted, she was on the phone.

He sighed, assuming she was on the phone with a 911 operator. The rest of the house contained two bedrooms, a hallway bath and master bath with a large garden tub. Candles were placed around it and their scents lingered in the air even though not lit. He cleared each of the rooms and closets. Convinced no one else was in the house, he returned to her.

Sirens blaring told him she'd called and they would be in the home within minutes. "The house is clear," he said as he placed the fire poker back in its place.

"Thank you," she managed with a shaky voice.

She stood in a royal blue dress that hugged every soft feminine curve of her body. The color brought out the red in her hair and the deep russet in her eyes. She was a beautiful woman, more so than any woman he'd laid eyes on. His urge was to take her in his arms and sweep her into his embrace. He suppressed the urge and grabbed her supple hand, caressing it in his. She gazed into his eyes.

The policeman rang the doorbell and hollered in a firm voice, "Ms. Rose."

"Come in, please," she responded, dropping his hand and entering the hallway.

The policeman introduced himself as John Neelmeger. He wasn't taller than five foot six, with a bell-shape. His

small eyes set inside a face of dough and thick salt and pepper hair greased back but not enough to cover the natural wave. He took Esma and Gracen aside as his partner checked the house and the paramedics confirmed the body was DOA.

Gracen didn't leave, but answered all the questions and listened while she responded to their inquiries. It was her boyfriend lying dead on the couch. There were no signs of forced entry and no marks or blood, nothing that gave any clues to how he died. After the autopsy they'd have a better clue what killed him, but they were assuming nature took its course early for him as he wasn't more than thirty.

Only an hour earlier they'd gotten into an argument and she left on a walk. That's when Gracen found her staring at the light, snowflakes diving from the sky and puddling around her boots. His heart leaped from his chest when he spotted her.

Her oval face and red pouty lips made it impossible for him not to reach out to her. "You can't stay here. Let me take you to a hotel."

Her russet eyes shifted, meeting his. "Thank you. Let me grab my coat."

He nodded and held her coat as she slipped her arms inside the sleeves and gracefully tugged her gloves over her hands and placed her hat on at an angle that drove him wild. He didn't place her over twenty-five, while he appeared at least fifteen years her senior.

The snow now inches high and still

falling would make the walk uncomfortable, so Gracen hailed a cab and the two squeezed into the back seat. She sat like a lady with her back straight against the seat and her hands folded in her lap.

"Stop at the Royale please," said Gracen to the driver. He turned and met her eyes. "Allow me to cover the cost."

"You've done so much already. I don't think I would have made it through everything without you there," she said in a demure voice.

He smiled. "It's my pleasure and I won't have

it any other way. A lady such as yourself shouldn't have to face such drama alone. I will check on you in the morning." He grabbed her hand and squeezed.

"Thank you, Mr. Halinger." She squeezed his hand in return and stepped out of the cab.

He watched as she entered the hotel and called the front desk, making sure she got the best room and putting her stay on his credit card.

He lay in bed that night unable to take his mind off her. Her eyes such a unique shade of brown, almost red mixed with her dark auburn hair, long legs and perfectly proportioned body she was a dream. His mind finally shut down enough for sleep to come but she didn't leave his thoughts.

Her soft hand took his and they walked backwards to the bed, their mouths met in a passionate kiss. Once they reached it she broke her lips away from his and unbuttoned his shirt, one by one, exposing his chest. She ran her fingers through the thin patch of wiry hair covering it, bringing her lips close she

dropped kisses on it
making a straight line
leading to his belt.
   An intense desire for
her raged inside him.
He'd never wanted a
woman so much and felt
an urgency to thrust
inside her but as a
gentleman he waited,
brushing his hands over
the back of her hair as she
unbuckled his belt and
worked the button and
his zipper, letting his
pants drop to the floor.
He tilted his head back,
his eyes staring sightless
at the smooth cream
ceiling as she engulfed his

penis with her moistened lips

Tenderly, he pushed her backwards onto the crimson satin duvet, lifting her cobalt gown over her luscious legs, displaying her nub and revealing a neatly trimmed patch of sleek dark auburn hair. He wanted nothing more than to please her as he brought his mouth to her clit and wiggled his tongue over it, sliding it in circles around the lips then driving it into her vagina. It was syrupy sweet like sucking on a cherry lollipop. Small moans of pleasure escaped her lips as her body jolted with the pleasure he brought her.

"I want you," she whispered, so quietly he barely heard it.

He guided his tongue across her belly and chest as he scooted forward on the bed until his hands rested beside her shoulders and his mouth met hers. He rested the tip of his cock at her moistened entrance and brushed lightly. Her hips met his movements, driving him over the edge. He fought his craving to plunge inside her. Building the desire, he inched inside her until her tight vagina swallowed him. The walls crushing against his cock as their bodies met in waves of pleasure, whimpers and moans breaking the silence in the air.

A sudden crash awoke him. Bolting upright, his sensuous dream faded but his dick throbbing and hard as a steel blade reminded him. Juices glistened from the tip to his groin. He swiped the liquid and brought it to his nose, inhaling in her scent, causing the blood in his body to pulse and rush further into his already swelling, hardened cock. Unconcerned and clueless how her juices left his dream, he brought his finger to his mouth and sucked her syrupy juices off it. He breathed heavy and crashed back onto his pillow. Wrapping his hand around his cock, he moved it quickly up and down to relieve the pressure building in his genitals. Cum squirted from the tip as another crash blasted his ears.